HORRiD HENRY'S
Homework

HORRiD HENRY'S
Homework

Francesca Simon

Illustrated by Tony Ross

Orion
Children's Books

Horrid Henry's Homework originally appeared in
Horrid Henry and the Mummy's Curse first published in
Great Britain in 2000 by Orion Children's Books
This edition first published in Great Britain in 2013
by Orion Children's Books
a division of the Orion Publishing Group Ltd
Orion House
5 Upper Saint Martin's Lane
London WC2H 9EA
An Hachette UK Company

1 3 5 7 9 10 8 6 4 2

ISBN 978 1 4440 0122 8
Printed in China

www.orionbooks.co.uk
www.horridhenry.co.uk

For our gorgeous boys,
Louis and Guy Levison,
love Mummy and Daddy

There are many more **Horrid Henry** books available.
For a complete list visit
www.horridhenry.co.uk
or
www.orionbooks.co.uk

Contents

Chapter 1

Ahhhh, thought Horrid Henry.

He turned on the TV
and stretched out. School was over.
What could be better than lying
on the sofa all afternoon,
eating crisps and watching TV?
Wasn't life grand?

Then Mum came in. She did not look like a mum who thought life was grand. She looked like a mum on the warpath against boys who lay on sofas all afternoon, eating crisps and watching TV.

"Get your feet off the sofa, Henry!"
said Mum.
"Unh," grunted Henry.

"Stop getting crisps everywhere!"
snapped Mum.
"Unh," grunted Henry.

"Have you done your homework,
Henry?" said Mum.
Henry didn't answer.

"Henry!" shouted Mum.

"What?" shouted Henry.

"Have you done your homework?"

"What homework?" said Henry.
He kept his eyes glued to the TV.
"Go, Mutants!" he screeched.

"The five spelling words you are meant to learn tonight," said Mum.

"Oh," said Henry.
"*That* homework."

Chapter 2

Horrid Henry hated homework.

He had far better things to do
with his precious time than learn
how to spell "zipper" or work out
the answer to 6 x 7.

For weeks Henry's homework sheets
had ended up in the recycling box
until Dad found them.

Henry swore he had no idea
how they got there and blamed
Fluffy the cat, but since then
Mum and Dad had checked his
school bag every day.

Mum snatched the zapper and
switched off the telly.

"Hey, I'm watching!" said Henry.

"When are you going to do your homework, Henry?" said Mum.

"Soon!" screamed Henry.

Chapter 3

He'd just returned from a long,
hard day at school. Couldn't he have
any peace around here?

When he was king anyone who said
the word "homework" would get
thrown to the crocodiles.

"I had a phone call today from
Miss Battle-Axe," said Mum.
"She said you got a zero in the
last ten spelling tests."

"That's not my fault," said Henry.
"First I lost the words, then I forgot,
then I couldn't read my writing,
then I copied the words wrong,
then…"

"I don't want to hear any more silly excuses," said Mum. "Do you know your spelling words for tomorrow?"

"Yes," lied Henry.

"Where's the list?" Mum asked.

"I don't know," said Henry.

"Find it or no TV for a month," said Mum.

"It's not fair," muttered Henry,
digging the crumpled spelling list
out of his pocket.
Mum looked at it.

"There's going to be a spelling test
tomorrow," she said
"How do you spell 'goat'?"

"Don't you know how, Mum?"
asked Henry.

"Henry…" said Mum.

Henry scowled.
"I'm busy," moaned Henry.
"I promise I'll tell you right
after Mutant Madman.
It's my favourite show."

"How do you spell 'goat'?"
snapped Mum.

"G–O–T–E," snapped Henry.

"Wrong," said Mum.

"What about 'boat'?"

"Why do I have to do this?"
wailed Henry.

"Because it's your homework,"
said Mum. "You have to learn
how to spell."

"But why?" said Henry.
"I never write letters."

"Because," said Mum.
"Now spell 'boat'."

"B–O–T–T–E," said Henry.

"No more TV until you do your homework," said Mum.

"I've done all my homework," said Perfect Peter. "In fact I enjoyed it so much I've already done tomorrow's homework as well."

Henry pounced on Peter.
He was a cannibal tenderising
his victim for the pot.

"Eeeeyowwww!"
screamed Peter.

"Henry! Go to your room!" shouted Mum. "And don't come out until you know *all* your spelling words!"

Chapter 4

Horrid Henry stomped upstairs
and slammed his bedroom door.
This was so unfair!

He was far too busy to bother with
stupid, boring, useless spelling.
For instance, he hadn't read the
New Mutant Madman comic book.

He hadn't finished drawing
that treasure map.

And he hadn't even begun to sort his new collection of Twizzle cards.

Homework would have to wait.

There was just one problem.
Miss Battle-Axe had said that
everyone who spelled all their words
correctly tomorrow would get
a pack of Big Bopper sweets.
Henry loved Big Bopper sweets.
Mum and Dad hardly ever
let him have them.

But why on earth did he have to learn spelling words to get some? If he were the teacher, he'd only give sweets to children who couldn't spell.

Henry sighed. He'd just have to sit down and learn those stupid words.

4.30.

Mum burst into the room.
Henry was lying on his bed
reading a comic.

"Henry! Why aren't you doing your homework?" said Mum.

"I'll do it in a sec," said Henry. "I'm just finishing this page.

"Henry…" said Mum.

Henry put down the comic.
Mum left.
Henry picked up the comic.

5.30.

Dad burst into the room.
Henry was playing with his knights.

"Henry! Why aren't you doing your homework?" said Dad.

"I'm tired," yawned Henry. "I'm just taking a little break. It's hard having so much work!"

"Henry, you've only got five words to learn!" said Dad. "And you've just spent two hours not learning them."

"All right," snarled Henry. Slowly, he picked up his spelling list.

Then he put it down again.
He had to get in the mood.
Soothing music,
that's what he needed.

Horrid Henry switched on his CD player. The terrible sound of the Driller Cannibals boomed through the house.

"Oh, I'm a
can-can-cannibal!"
screamed Henry,
stomping around his room.
"Don't call me an
animal just 'cause
I'm a can-can-
cannibal!"

Chapter 5

Mum and Dad stormed into
Henry's bedroom and turned off
the music.

"That's enough, Henry!" said Dad.

"Do your homework!"
screamed Mum.

"If you don't get every single word
right in your test tomorrow there
will be no television for a week!"
shouted Dad.

Eeek! No TV and no sweets!
This was too much.

Horrid Henry looked at his spelling
words with loathing.

goat

boat

said

stoat

friend

"I hate goats! I'll never need to spell
the word 'goat' in my life,"
said Henry.

He hated goat's cheese.
He hated goat's milk.
He thought goats were smelly.
That was one word he'd never
need to know.

The next word was "boat".

Who needs to spell that? thought
Henry. I'm not going to be a sailor
when I grow up. I get seasick.
In fact, it's bad for my health to learn
how to spell "boat".

As for "said", what did it matter if
he spelt it "sed"? It was perfectly
understandable, written "sed".
Only an old fusspot like
Miss Battle-Axe would mind
such a tiny mistake.

Then there was "stoat".
What on earth was a stoat?
What a mean, sneaky word.
Henry wouldn't know a stoat
if it sat on him.

Of all the useless, horrible words,
"stoat" was the worst.
Trust his teacher, Miss Battle-Axe,
to make him learn a horrible,
useless word like stoat.

The last word was "friend".
Well, a real friend like Rude Ralph
didn't care how the word "friend"
was spelt. As far as Henry was
concerned any friend who minded
how he spelt "friend" was no friend.
Miss Battle-Axe included that word
to torture him.

Five whole spelling words.
It was too much. I'll never learn
so many words, thought Henry.
But what about tomorrow?
He'd have to watch Moody Margaret
and Jolly Josh and Clever Clare
chomping away at those delicious
Big Boppers, while he, Henry,
had to gnash his empty teeth.

Plus no TV for a week! Henry
couldn't live that long without TV!
He was sunk.
He was doomed to be sweetless,
and TV-less.

But wait.
What if there was a way to get
those sweets without the horrid
hassle of learning to spell?

Chapter 6

Suddenly, Henry had a brilliant, spectacular idea. It was so simple Henry couldn't believe he'd never thought of it before.

He sat next to Clever Clare. Clare always knew the spelling words. All Henry had to do was to take a little peek at her work.

If he positioned his chair right, he'd easily be able to see what she wrote. And he wouldn't be copying her, no way. Just double-checking.

I am a genius, thought Horrid
Henry. 100% right on the test.
Loads of Big Bopper sweets.
Mum and Dad would be so thrilled
they'd let him watch extra TV.

Hurray!

Horrid Henry swaggered into
class the next morning.
He sat down in his seat between
Clever Clare and Beefy Bert.
Carefully, he inched his chair over
a fraction so that he had a
good view of Clare's paper.

"Spelling test!" barked Miss Battle-Axe. "First word – goat."

Clare bent over her paper. Henry pretended he was staring at the wall, then, quick as a flash, he glanced at her work and wrote "goat".

"Boat," said Miss Battle-Axe. Again, Horrid Henry sneaked a look at Clare's paper and copied her.

And again.

And again.

This is fantastic, thought Henry. I'll never have to learn any spelling words. Just think of all the comic books he could read instead of wasting his time on homework!

He sneaked a peak at Beefy Bert's paper. Blank. Ha ha, thought Henry.

There was only one word left. Henry could taste the tingly tang of a Big Bopper already. Wouldn't he swagger about! And no way would he share his sweets with anyone.

Suddenly, Clare shifted position
and edged away from him. Rats!
Henry couldn't see her paper
any more.

"Last word," boomed
Miss Battle-Axe. "Friend."

Henry twisted in his seat.
He could see the first four words.
He just needed to get
a tiny bit closer...

Clare looked at him. Henry stared at the ceiling. Clare glared, then looked back at her paper. Quickly, Henry leaned over and … Yes! He copied down the final word, "friend".

Victory!

Chomp!

Chomp!

Chomp!

Hmmnn, boy,
did those Big Boppers taste great.

Someone tapped him on the
shoulder. It was Miss Battle-Axe.
She was smiling at him with her
great big yellow teeth.
Miss Battle-Axe had never smiled
at Henry before.

"Well, Henry," said Miss Battle-Axe.
"What an improvement! I'm thrilled."

"Thank you," said Henry modestly.

"In fact, you've done so well I'm promoting you to the top spelling group. Twenty-five extra words a night. Here's the list."

Horrid Henry's jaws stopped chomping. He looked in horror at the new spelling list. It was littered with words. But not just any words.

Awful words.

Mean words.

Long words.

Hard words.

hirowgleer

Hieroglyphs.

hirogix

Trapezium.

trepeezim

Diarrhoea.

diaryah

dioreahh

"Aaaaahhhhhhhhhhh!"
shrieked Horrid Henry.

What are you going to read next?

More adventures with Horrid Henry,

or go exploring with Shumba,

and brave the Jungle and Arctic with Algy.

Find a frog prince with Tulsa

or even a big, yellow, whiskery

Lion in the Meadow!

Tuck into some

Blood and Guts and
Rats' Tail Pizza,

learn to dance with
Sophie,

travel back
in time with

Cudweed

and sail away in

Noah's Ark.

Enjoy all the Early Readers.

Collect all the
Horrid Henry storybooks!

Horrid Henry

Horrid Henry
and the Secret Club

Horrid Henry Tricks the
Tooth Fairy

Horrid Henry
Gets Rich Quick

Horrid Henry's Nits

Horrid Henry's Haunted
House

Horrid Henry and
the Mummy's Curse

Horrid Henry's
Revenge

Horrid Henry and the
Bogey Babysitter

Horrid Henry's Stinkbomb

the orion star

Sign up for  the orion star newsletter
for all the latest children's book news,
plus activity sheets, exclusive competitions,
author interviews, pre-publication extracts
and more.

www.orionbooks.co.uk/newsletters

Follow @the_orionstar on  .